Magic with Grace

"For Harper and Emma - who truly bring magic into my life."

Magic with Grace

Published by: Hidden Castle Books

Layout and Design by Andy Grachuk
www.JingotheCat.com

This book belongs to.....

_____

———— ❧ ————

Long, long ago, in a faraway place,
Lived a family of wizards, with a daughter named Grace.
Her hair was brown and her eyes were blue,
She was missing a tooth and wore a tutu.

Her parents were famous and loved by all,
For their magic helped people both big and small.
With a wave of their wands and a smile on their face,
There was not a problem they could not erase.

———— ❧ ————

4

But Grace had a problem that would not go away,
Day after day IT would get in her way.
It was noisy and smelly and skipped on the floor,
It was nosey and annoying and loved to explore.

But try as she might, Grace could not sway her mother,
To wave that magic wand and get rid of her little brother!
"Jack is sweet and just wants to play."
"Be a good older sister and take him outside today."

6

With a huff and a twirl, Grace threw up her hands,
"Fine he can come, he won't ruin my plans!"
She pulled out her wand and waved it with pride,
"I summon Mr. Fuzzy to give Jack a ride!"

In a big puff of smoke, Mr. Fuzzy appeared,
He was huge, he was hairy, and he had a long beard.
He purred with excitement as he rubbed against Jack,
Then took him by the shirt and flipped him on to his back.

They raced out the door and onto the lawn,
Grace came to a stop and shouted "Hold on!"
"The game we will play is hide-and-go-seek."
"I will count to ten and promise not to peek."

So Grace started counting while Jack skipped away,
Mr. Fuzzy walked in circles, confused how to play.
"One... two... three... four..."
Mr. Fuzzy laid down and started to snore.

11

"Five... six... seven... eight..."
Jack smiled and laughed as he made his escape.
"Nine... TEN!" Grace said with a shout,
She opened her eyes and stared all about.

She saw Mr. Fuzzy asleep on the ground,
Then tagged him on the head and said "One found!"
Grace looked all around as she tried to spot Jack,
But try as she might, she could not find his track.

13

He was not in the bushes or up in the sky,
He was not behind the statue or in a tree way up high.
"Oh no I've lost Jack! Where can he be?"
"Jack, come out now, this isn't funny!"

Then all of a sudden, someone started to giggle,
Mr. Fuzzy was asleep, but his beard began to wiggle.
Grace narrowed her eyes and started to grin,
She waved her magic wand and said "Leva-ka-zin!"

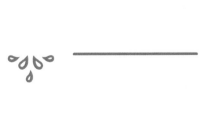

A magical cloud lifted Mr. Fuzzy high,
Revealing Jack underneath, peeking out with one eye.
Grace ran over to Jack and tagged him with tickles,
"If you scare me like that again, I'll make you eat pickles!"

They laughed with each other and went back inside,
While their parents looked on, beaming with pride.
"They play well together," mother said with a sigh.
"Should we tell them Mr. Fuzzy's still up in the sky?"

Make Your Own Adventure!

Color the pictures and fill in the <u>blanks</u>

on the following pages to create your own

Wizard Adventure!

title: _____

by: _____

Long, long ago, in a faraway _____,
Lived a family of wizards, with a daughter named _____.
Her hair was _____ and her eyes were _____,
She was missing a _____ and wore a _____.

Her parents were famous and loved by all,
For their magic helped people both big and small.
With a wave of their wands and a smile on their face,
There was not a problem they could not erase.

But _____ had a problem that would not go away,

Day after day IT would get in her way.

It was _____ and _____ and _____ on the floor,

It was _____ and _____ and loved to explore.

But try as she might, _____ could not sway her mother,

To wave that magic wand and get rid of her little brother!

"_____ is sweet and just wants to play."

"Be a good older sister and take him outside today."

——————— ⟡ ———————

With a huff and a twirl, _____ threw up her hands,
"Fine he can come, he won't ruin my plans!"
She pulled out her wand and waved it with pride,
"I summon _____ to give _____ a ride!"

In a big puff of smoke, _____ appeared,
He was _____, he was _____, and he had a long beard.
He purred with excitement as he rubbed against _____,
Then took him by the shirt and flipped him on to his _____.

——————— ⟡ ———————

They raced out the door and onto the lawn,

_____ came to a stop and shouted "Hold on!"

"The game we will play is hide-and-go-seek."

"I will count to ten and promise not to peek."

So _____ started counting while _____ skipped away,

_____ walked in circles, confused how to play.

"One... two... three... four..."

_____ laid down and started to snore.

"Five... six... seven... eight..."
_____ smiled and laughed as he made his escape.
"Nine... TEN!" _____ said with a shout,
She opened her eyes and stared all about.

She saw _____ asleep on the ground,
Then tagged him on the head and said "One found!"
_____ looked all around as she tried to spot _____,
But try as she might, she could not find his track.

———————— ✿ ————————

He was not in the bushes or up in the sky,
He was not behind the statue or in a tree way up high.
"Oh no I've lost _____! Where can he be?"
"_____, come out now, this isn't funny!"

Then all of a sudden, someone started to giggle,
_____ was asleep, but his beard began to wiggle.
_____ narrowed her eyes and started to grin,
She waved her magic wand and said "_____!"

———————— ✿ ————————

——————— ⚬ᦢᦢᦢ ———————

A magical cloud lifted _____ high,
Revealing _____ underneath, peeking out with one eye.
_____ ran over to _____ and tagged him with ____,
"If you scare me like that again, I'll make you eat _____!"

They laughed with each other and went back inside,
While their parents looked on, beaming with pride.
"They play well together," mother said with a sigh.
"Should we tell them _____ still up in the sky?"

——————— ᦢᦢᦢ ———————

The End

Made in the USA
Monee, IL
19 December 2020